The Battle
for
Christmas

JoEllen Claypool

For more information, please contact:
Valley Walker Press
P.O. Box 164
New Plymouth, ID 83655
joclaypool@hotmail.com
First printing 2016

ISBN – 978-0-9857658-6-6
Library of Congress Control Number - 2016911022

To order additional copies of this book, contact Valley Walker Press at the address listed above.

DEDICATION

I dedicate this book to my beautiful mother, JoAnn Biesheuvel,
who assigned the topic and challenged me to write this poem in two days
for her annual cookie party, which then worked into being
a perfect idea for my first children's book.
Thank you, Mom, for believing in me!

Children and adults alike can have fun with all of the **RIGHTS** that are **LEFT** in this book...or all of the **LEFTS** that are **RIGHT** in this book. You can incorporate this story into learning time, game time, or anytime! Whatever activities you choose, use the **RIGHT** and **LEFT** cues to change direction or alternate the hands and feet that are being used. Here is a list of ideas to get you started:

- Stand in a circle with all **RIGHT** hands in the middle. Circle around as the teacher reads the book until you come to a **LEFT**, then change hands and circle the other way.
- Start hopping on your **RIGHT** foot and change feet when you hear the word **LEFT.**
- Play hot potato, starting by tossing it to anyone on your **RIGHT**. Listen closely because when you hear the word **LEFT**, you must start passing it to any person on the left.
- Grab a partner and face each other. When you hear the word **RIGHT**, give each other a high five with your right hand. When you hear the word **LEFT**, give each other a high five with your left hand.
- Get silly! Grab a partner and lay on your backs with your legs bent and your feet facing your partner's feet. Give each other high fives with your feet! Touch right feet when you hear the word **RIGHT** and left feet when you hear the word **LEFT.**
- Have a drawing game. List some simple items to draw (candy cane, present, tree, etc.). When you hear the word **RIGHT**, draw the item on the list with your right hand. When you hear the word **LEFT**, draw the next item on the list with your left hand.
- This book has been used at a gift exchange. **RIGHT** and **LEFT** would be used to determine which direction the gift was passed. Whichever gift you are holding at the end of the book is the gift you get to open.
- Use your imagination to come up with your own ideas for games and activities!

Sit **RIGHT** down
and listen to this.
It's a tale of three holidays
battling for Christmas.

It starts in the workshop
with the elves all at work.
Two shady characters
by the window did lurk.

Pete Pumpkin was on the **LEFT**
with his eyes aglow
and Tom Turkey on the **RIGHT**
with his wattle hung low.

They had to be patient
and time it just **RIGHT**,
but what they were attempting
would be quite the sight.

With the window opened wide,
they saw their chance.
So as not to be conspicuous,
they pretended to dance.

Pete Pumpkin wobbled
and tried not to fall down.
"I've got two **LEFT** feet!"
gobbled Tom, stumbling around.

"Just grab the **RIGHT** gifts!
They're **RIGHT** on the table!"
Tom waltzed **LEFT** then **RIGHT**,
feeling less than stable.

They both met at the edge
with eyes opened wide.
They huffed and puffed
as they still tried to hide.

Then they both gasped
at the sight they saw-
Santa in a snow globe!
They each dropped their jaw.

"Santa's been caught!" Pete said
RIGHT off the bat
then looked at Tom and said,
"I'd give your **LEFT** wing for that."

"Are you in your **RIGHT** mind?"
Tom gave him the eye.
"Santa's not that small!
That globe is a lie!"

"He's an elf all **RIGHT**
but all big and jolly.
So get your head on **RIGHT**,
and don't be **LEFT** in your folly."

"We must be quick,
and we must be wise
because on Santa's side,
he's definitely got size."

"**RIGHT** on, Turkey.
I dig what you're sayin'.
Let's grab some gifts,
so we can start playin'."

"Which ones do you want?"
came a voice **RIGHT** above.
It was a deep voice but gentle,
one filled with love.

They both turned around,
and each lifted his head.
All thoughts they were having
were all **LEFT** unsaid.

He stood **RIGHT** there
in his red, white, and black.
To the **LEFT** of him sat
his overstuffed toy sack.

"No **LEFT**overs for you.
I'll let you choose first."
Pete Pumpkin was so excited,
he thought he would burst.

Tom was still skeptical
and not sure he'd heard **RIGHT**.
He carefully approached
and gazed at Santa's height.

"Step **RIGHT** up,
Tom Turkey. Come here.
Don't be **LEFT** behind.
You have nothing to fear."

"Now tell me, you two,
why'd you come to my home?
Were you coming to visit,
or did you come just to roam?"

"We wanted your gifts
and the joy that you hold
to bring **RIGHT** back to our
holidays and make them as bold."

"Mine has a bad rap,"
said Pete sadly.
"I want bright colored boxes
and bows so badly."

"I want fun music **LEFT**
on all day and all night
and cookies **LEFT** out
instead of a fright."

Then Tom spoke **RIGHT** up
and **LEFT** his pal's side.
He flew up to Santa's shoulder
with one smooth glide.

Now eye to eye,
Tom spoke with sincerity.
"My reason is purely selfish,"
he said with clarity.

"I want a nice gift
LEFT to distract,
one to keep me
from being attacked."

"**RIGHTLY** so!"
said Santa, upset.
"Let me think for a moment
and see what we can get."

"I'll be **RIGHT** back!"
He set out on two tasks.
Santa **LEFT** the building
then came back with two masks.

To Pete, he handed
a bright feathered design.
Pete's gapped grin spoke,
"Yes, this is **RIGHT** fine."

To Tom, he handed
a raven disguise.
Tom gobbled and giggled
and thought Santa quite wise.

Before they **LEFT**, Tom said,
"We want you to know.
We'd plant a kiss on your cheek,
if we had a mistletoe."

"Is that **RIGHT**? Ho, ho, ho!"
Santa laughed.
"You both are so silly,
you both are so daft."

Pete asked, "But why were you so kind,
when our hearts were so bad?"
"Two wrongs don't make a **RIGHT**," Santa
said to the lad.

RIGHT in the nick of time,
Santa saved the day
with his jolly soul
and his gentle way.

There was no time **LEFT**.
They had to move **RIGHT** along
to their respective holidays,
where each did belong.

GLOSSARY

Clarity – the quality of being clear

Conspicuous – attracting notice or attention

Daft – silly; foolish

Lurk – to move in a secret way so you cannot be seen

Respective – belonging to each one of the things that have been mentioned

Sincerity – truthfulness

Skeptical – suspicious; doubtful

Wattle - a fleshy lobe or appendage hanging down from the throat or chin of certain birds such as the chicken or turkey.

ABOUT THE AUTHOR

JoEllen Claypool lives in Idaho where she enjoys her life as a homeschooling mom and a pastor's wife. Her spare time consists of helping others achieve their dreams of becoming authors. She provides one-on-one instruction as a book coach and provides opportunities for writers through events that she and three other authors facilitate through the Idaho Creative Authors Network (I CAN). JoEllen loves stretching herself in her writing by exploring poetry, children's books, fiction, and nonfiction. She wants others to understand that everyone has a story to write no matter how old you are!